بسم الله الرحمن الرحيم

Adventures in the Nile Valley

Susan Omar

The Islamic Foundation

ISBN 0 86037 242 1

MUSLIM CHILDREN'S LIBRARY

General Editors:
M. Manazir Ahsan and **Anwar Cara**

ADVENTURES IN THE NILE VALLEY

Author: **Susan Omar**
Art Work: **Abdullah Nait Attia**

Published by
The Islamic Foundation
Markfield Dawah Centre
Ratby Lane, Markfield
Leicester LE67 9RN, UK

Quran House
PO Box 30611
Nairobi, Kenya

PMB 3193
Kano, Nigeria

Printed and bound by
Cromwell Press Limited, Melksham, Wiltshire

With grateful thanks to my husband, Tarek,
and my parents, Bryan and Pat Pickering
for their advice and encouragement.

Also thanks to Al-Qur'an Society, London
for supplying, at short notice,
material on Imām Shāfi'ī.

Susan Omar

Transliteration

Guide to pronouncing Arabic Words

For some Arabic vowels and sounds there is no English equivalent. In order to help readers overcome this problem some special marks have been put on certain words in this book.

For example, ā, ī and ū stand for the vowel sounds aa (as in path), ee (as in feet) and oo (as in pool) respectively.

Similarly, the signs (’) and (‘) have been used for the Arabic letter ‘hamza’ (as in *Wuḍū’*) and ‘ ‘ayn’ (as in *Ka‘bah*).

Arabic Alphabet and its English Equivalent

ء	’	د	d	ض	ḍ	ك	k
ب	b	ذ	dh	ط	ṭ	ل	l
ت	t	ر	r	ظ	ẓ	م	m
ث	th	ز	z	ع	‘	ن	n
ج	j	س	s	غ	gh	ه	h
ح	ḥ	ش	sh	ف	f	و	w
خ	kh	ص	ṣ	ق	q	ي	y

MUSLIM CHILDREN'S LIBRARY

An Introduction

Here is a new series of books, but with a difference, for children of all ages. Published by the Islamic Foundation, the Muslim Children's Library has been produced to provide young people with something they cannot perhaps find anywhere else.

Most of today's children's books aim only to entertain and inform or to teach some necessary skills, but not to develop the inner and moral resources. Entertainment and skills by themselves impart nothing of value to life unless a child is also helped to discover deeper meaning in himself and the world around him. Yet there is no place in them for God, Who alone gives meaning to life and the universe, nor for the divine guidance brought by His prophets, following which can alone ensure an integrated development of the total personality.

Such books, in fact, rob young people of access to true knowledge. They give them no unchanging standards of right and wrong, nor any incentives to live by what is right and refrain from what is wrong. The result is that all too often the young enter adult life in a state of social alienation and bewilderment, unable to cope with the seemingly unlimited choices of the world around them. The situation is especially devastating for the Muslim child as he may grow up cut off from his culture and values.

The Muslim Children's Library aspires to remedy this deficiency by showing children the deeper meaning of life and the world around them; by pointing them along paths leading to an integrated development of all aspects of their personality; by helping to give them the capacity to cope with the complexities of their world, both personal and social; by opening vistas into a world extending far beyond this life; and, to a Muslim child especially, by providing a fresh and strong faith, a dynamic commitment, an indelible sense of identity, a throbbing yearning and an urge to struggle, all rooted in Islam. The books aim to help a child anchor his development on the rock of divine guidance, and to understand himself and relate to himself and others in just and meaningful ways. They relate directly to his soul and intellect, to his emotions and imagination, to his motives and desires, to his anxieties and hopes – indeed, to every aspect of his fragile, but potentially rich personality. At the same time it is recognized that for a book to hold a child's attention, he must enjoy reading it; it should therefore arouse his curiosity and entertain him as well. The style, the language, the illustrations and the production of the books are all geared to this goal. They provide moral education, but not through sermons or ethical abstractions.

Although these books are based entirely on Islamic teachings and the vast Muslim heritage, they should be of equal interest and value to all children, whatever their country or creed; for Islam is a universal religion, the natural path.

Adults, too, may find much of use in them. In particular, Muslim parents and teachers will find that they provide what they have for so long been so badly needing. The books will include texts on the Qur'ān, the *Sunnah* and other basic sources and teachings of Islam, as well as history, stories and anecdotes for supplementary reading. The books are presented with full colour illustrations keeping in view the limitations set by Islam. As a companion volume to *New Friends, New Places* the present book, *Adventures in the Nile Valley*, presents a fascinating account of the British Muslim boy Adam's second visit to Egypt. His travels take him to many exciting historical places and Islamic monuments, and give him an opportunity to observe and participate in many Islamic activities, reinforcing his commitment to Islam and giving him a sense of pride in being a Muslim and belonging to the universal *Ummah* (community) of Islam.

We invite parents and teachers to use these books in homes and classrooms, at breakfast tables and bedsides and encourage children to derive maximum benefit from them. At the same time their greatly valued observations and suggestions are highly welcome.

To the young reader we say: You hold in your hands books which may be entirely different from those you have been reading till now, but we sincerely hope you will enjoy them; try, through these books, to understand yourself, your life, your experiences and the universe around you. They will open before your eyes new paths and models in life that you will be curious to explore and find exciting and rewarding to follow. May God be with you forever.

We are grateful to everyone who has helped in the publication of this book, particularly Dr. A.R. Kidwai and Br. Anwar Cara, who read *Adventures in the Nile Valley* with great interest and offered valuable suggestions.

May Allah bless with His mercy and acceptance our humble contribution to the urgent and gigantic task of producing books for a new generation of children, a task which we have undertaken in all humility and hope.

M. Manazir Ahsan
Director General

1

An unexpected excursion

'So we're off to the pyramids!' said Adam in excitement. 'I've always wanted to see the pyramids of Egypt!'

'Then today's your lucky day,' laughed the driver, dodging his taxi in and out of rows of crowded buses.

Adam watched as Sha'bān, the taxi driver, lit a stick of incense and set it on the dashboard next to an open copy of the Holy Qur'ān. As the incense smoke wafted round the taxi, making it hard to see out of the already dusty windscreen, Adam thought how nice it was to be back in Egypt.

English-born Adam was enjoying his second holiday in Egypt* with his parents and baby sister Nadia. They were staying in Cairo with his Father's Egyptian relatives, among them Adam's cousins Muhammad and Ahmad.

The taxi driver suddenly leaned out of the window to hail a friend.

' 'Alī!' he shouted. 'Hop in, friend!' Even before the taxi had come to a halt, a young man carrying a bundle of books had detached himself from the crowds of pedestrians and jumped in beside Adam and Ahmad.

'*As-salāmu 'alaikum* (peace be with you),' he said. 'I'm 'Alī.'

---

*Adam's first visit to Egypt is described in *New Friends, New Places,* published by the Islamic Foundation in 1993.

'Wa'alaikum as-salām (peace be with you too),' replied Adam and his cousins together, returning the Islamic greeting of peace and shaking 'Alī's hand.

'Where are you boys heading for?' asked 'Alī easily, stretching his legs. 'Mind if you drop me off at the *Madrasah* on the way?'

'No, that's no problem,' announced Sha'bān, casually rearranging the boys' plans for them. 'We were going to the pyramids, but never mind them now. Now 'Alī, you can show my young friends here round your *Madrasah*. Ah! Isn't that Qārī Bāsiṭ 'Abdus Ṣamad?'

Adam, by now quite confused, looked around, expecting another friend to jump into the taxi. Anything seemed possible here. But no, Bāsiṭ 'Abdus Ṣamad was apparently the Qur'ān reader on the radio.

'He is one of the greatest Qur'ān reciters in Egypt, you know!' said 'Alī, dropping his books as the taxi took a sudden swing down a narrow lane. 'Hey, mind that donkey, Sha'bān! Yes – I'll be pleased to show you round my University – the *Madrasah*. It's another of Egypt's "greatest" you know. We say that it's the greatest university in the Middle East.'

'Thanks 'Alī,' said Adam, but, turning to cousin Muhammad in the front seat he asked anxiously, 'But what about seeing the pyramids and the great sphinx?'

'*Mā lish* – never mind,' said Muhammad with a shrug. 'They've been standing there for more than 4000 years already you know, Adam. *Inshā' Allāh,* they'll still be there tomorrow!'

Just then the taxi came to a jolting halt. 'Here we are, this is the famous Madrasah Al-Azhar ash-Sharīf,' said 'Alī. The three boys jumped out and followed the tall student across a large courtyard and through a gateway. The university looked like a castle.

'That's the main university library through there,' said 'Alī, indicating a large door. That's where I spend hours studying.' As they walked through a maze of courtyards surrounded by elegant pillars, 'Alī told the boys that he was studying Islamic Law which is called *Sharī'ah.* 'I want to be a writer on Islamic Affairs when I've finished my studies,' he told them proudly. He was very enthusiastic about Al-Azhar University, telling them that it had originally been built by rulers of Egypt called Fātimids hundreds of years ago, and he pointed out the high minarets soaring above the buildings and the beautiful artwork on the walls. They reached a large hall where a number of girls were sitting cross-legged on mats around a religious teacher, swaying back and forth as they chanted in unison chapters, or *sūrahs,* from the Qur'ān.

'The girls are from poor families in Cairo,' explained 'Alī. 'They come here for free lessons so that they can read and understand the Qur'ān. I'm sure you know that Islam emphasizes the importance of education and knowledge for all Muslim people.'

Standing by the giant stone pillars in the huge hall, teachers were lecturing to groups of students sitting on the floor around them, busily taking notes. During the lessons, which the boys could only hear as a dim

murmur, some students would get up and join other student circles nearby. There were lots of lessons going on at the same time, and Adam wondered what the students were learning about. The *Madrasah* was certainly nothing like his school in England. They tiptoed out of the chamber and walked along a cool, dark passage where only the whirring of overhead fans disturbed the silence.

'Isn't the Al-Azhar University nice and quiet compared to the rest of Cairo,' remarked Ahmad.

'Absolutely, and students need peace and quiet to concentrate properly,' laughed 'Alī.

'What do you concentrate on?' asked Ahmad.

'Oh, our studies generally, like you do at school,' answered 'Alī. 'We also turn our minds to our duties towards Allah and develop self control, especially at the moment, as it is the month of Ramaḍān.'

Ahmad knew that during the Muslim month of Ramaḍān it is the duty of every grown-up Muslim (with a few exceptions) to go without food and drink from dawn to sunset. This is one of the five pillars of Islam.

'I've noticed that restaurants and snack stalls are closed all over Cairo,' remarked Adam.

'Ah – yes. That happens in all Muslim countries throughout Ramaḍān,' 'Alī told them. 'There's no food until after *Ṣalāt al-Maghrib* in the evening. Because tomorrow is the last day of Ramaḍān, *Inshā' Allāh* there will be great celebrations in the evening. Until then we can feel what it is like to have empty stomachs. *Inshā' Allāh* we will have more feeling for the poor people of the world who are often hungry.'

Just then, from the tops of mosque towers – or minarets – all over Cairo came the beautiful voices of men called Muezzins, calling everyone to prayer.

'*Allāhu Akbar*!' came the calls, some from the five minarets of the university.

'Come with me to pray in the Al-Azhar Mosque,' invited 'Alī at once. 'I'll show you where to do *Wuḍū'*.' *Wuḍū'* is the special way to wash oneself before praying to Allah, and there were crowds of white-robed students already performing *Wuḍū'* in small fountains in the washing courtyard. 'Alī kept an eye on the boys to make sure that they followed the procedure correctly, washing first the hands to the wrists three times, then the mouth and nose three times and the face three times, followed by the right arm to the elbow, then the left, each three times, before running wet hands over the head once and, finally, washing three times first the right foot and then the left.

A group of tourists was milling round the main door, hoping to look inside the Mosque, but the man looking after the worshippers' shoes politely asked them to leave, as they were not dressed suitably for a place of worship.

'It's not right for tourists to come into a Mosque wearing T-shirts and shorts,' whispered 'Alī. 'It doesn't show respect.'

The boys left their shoes at the door and followed 'Alī into the main hall of the Mosque. It was the largest Mosque Adam had ever seen, and very beautiful, with rows and rows of arches and columns. 'Alī led them to a space among the lines of Muslims where they lined up quietly. When the Muezzin's calls had finished, the main *Ṣalāt* (prayers) began. Facing the *Miḥrāb,* the direction of Makkah, Adam quietly followed the *Imām* as he led the prayer. Alongside Adam were his cousins and 'Alī and hundreds of Al-Azhar students, all as one as they offered their prayers to Allah.

When the prayer was over, Adam tried to read the swirling Arabic letters carved in wood above one of the niches. It said:

> In the Name of Allah, the Merciful, the Compassionate, be watchful over the Prayers, and over praying with the utmost excellence, and stand before Allah as would utterly obedient servants.

'Alī later told Adam that this was a quotation from the Qur'ān (*Sūrah al-Baqarah* 2: 238).

2

Out and about in Cairo

Adam's sleep that night was interrupted by a drumming noise which became louder and more demanding. 'Wake up! Leave your sleep!' cried a loud voice outside the apartment. 'It's time to declare that Allah is One and it's time to eat! Wake up!' It was the man known as a *Musahharatī*, beating on a drum and urging everyone in the neighbourhood to eat and pray before the day's fasting began at dawn. Every night of the Muslim month of Ramaḍān the *Musahharatīs* conducted the same ritual, but as this was the last night of Ramaḍān, the drums were louder and the cries more urgent.

Adam wandered into the kitchen to see what they were going to eat, his hair still rumpled from sleep. Muhammad and Ahmad appeared from their apartment next door, carrying some freshly fried *ta'miyah* (mashed beans) cooked by their mother Samirah, and soon they were joined by all the other relatives. Grandmother said a prayer of thanks to Allah for the food, and they started to eat.

Ahmad and Muhammad were in good spirits, planning the next evening's celebrations to mark *'Īd al-Fiṭr* – the festival that comes at the end of Ramaḍān each year.

'You're a bit quiet, Adam,' remarked Muhammad.

'I'm just tired,' yawned Adam.

'Never mind,' said Father kindly. 'You can go back to sleep after the prayers.'

Mother stayed behind looking after Adam's baby sister Nadia, while the rest of the family congregated at the nearest Mosque for *Ṣalāt al-Fajr.* Adam decided to stay where he was to say *Tasbīḥ* (praising Allah) to himself after the prayers. 'Alī had told him that Muslims may, if they wish to, say *Tasbīḥ* after every *Ṣalāh.* Adam counted on his fingers as he said to himself '*Subḥān Allah* – Glory be to Allah' thirty-three times, and then '*Al-Ḥamdulillāh* – Praise be to Allah' thirty-three times and lastly '*Allāhu Akbar* – Allah is Great' thirty-four times.

In the morning, Adam went with his cousins and Uncle Khalid to deliver some messages in the city. They took an underground metro train to Tāhir Square, near the great River Nile.

'I've got to send a fax to a camel driver up in the Western Desert for the next part of your trip,' said Uncle Khalid. 'It shouldn't take long.' It was odd how, whenever Uncle Khalid said something shouldn't take long, it always seemed to take for ever. The huge administration building that Uncle Khalid led them to was already overflowing with queues of people. Surely they weren't all waiting to use the fax machine? After battling their way along crowded corridors, they eventually found the fax office, but it was closed.

'Is it always this crowded in the Mujamma' Building?' asked Adam. 'It's getting awfully hot.'

'Don't worry. *Inshā' Allāh,* the fax office will open in a minute,' said Uncle Khalid airily.

'I hope it will, because we've arranged to meet Mother at the Mosque of Imām Shāfi'ī later,' said Adam. At last a lady came to open the office, but Uncle Khalid couldn't get his fax through. Unconcerned by this, he left his message with the clerk, who promised to try to send the fax later in the day.

'We'll call back later and see if there's a reply,' said Uncle Khalid to his nephews, and they all trooped out of the hot, crowded building. The raised footpaths round Tāhir Square were also jammed with people. The boys had to hang onto their uncle's robe to avoid getting separated in the crowd. Their next task should have been to collect some documents for Father from the printer, but Uncle Khalid remembered that they were near to the famous Egyptian Museum of Antiquities and couldn't resist taking the boys to see it.

'You can't visit Cairo without seeing the treasures of Tutankhamun and the Pharaohs,' he said enthusiastically. 'It won't take long.' Adam looked at his watch.

'We don't want to be late,' he warned, but Uncle Khalid was already disappearing into the crowd at a brisk walk, his white *Jallābiyah* – Arab robe – flowing behind him. The Egyptian Museum turned out to be fascinating. Muhammad took out his camera to photograph the gold face-mask of the boy king Tutankhamun, but he was at once stopped by a security guard who told him that photographs were not allowed.

'Whew, I thought for a minute he was going to take my camera away,' said Muhammad.

Later they filtered out into the sunshine and sat by the fountain, reflecting on the great civilization of Ancient Egypt when Ramses and Akenkaten and other kings ruled and organized the building of the pyramids.

'You boys look tired, so why don't you stay here and I'll just nip back to the Mujamma' Building to see about that fax,' suggested Uncle Khalid. 'I won't be long,' he added, and Adam's heart sank at the familiar words. They read the pamphlets about the museum and talked to some Swedish tourists who were interested to find that Adam could speak both English and Arabic. Yet after an hour there was still no sign of Uncle Khalid.

'We've waited long enough, haven't we?' complained Ahmad. 'It's really dusty here and I'm tired. Can't we head back to the apartments?'

They were still discussing what to do when Uncle Khalid returned.

'Oh, you're still here,' he said, seemingly in surprise. 'I thought you would have gone home by now.'

'Why would we do that when you've promised to take us to the Mosque of Imām Shāfi'ī?' asked Adam. 'We've been waiting an hour now.' With the heat and the deafening noise of traffic added to their hunger and thirst, everyone's nerves were rather frayed and they were losing patience with one another. After hailing a taxi, they found to their dismay that the traffic was almost at a standstill. At a busy junction, a policeman was trying to direct the traffic, but the drivers seemed to be taking no notice. Cars, taxis and buses swarmed forward from every

direction, while pedestrians, many of them carrying baskets on their heads, stepped out into the road as if immune from danger. Horns were hooting and fumes filled the air. Adam wished he could wind up the taxi window, but there was no handle.

It took so long to get going that Adam was worrying about being late meeting Mother. Uncle Khalid told him that she would have gone home without waiting for them, but Adam shook his head.

'Really, Uncle Khalid,' he complained. 'You don't seem to take appointments seriously at all!'

At last they arrived at the Mausoleum and Mosque of Imām Shāfi'ī and there, sure enough, was Mother, holding baby Nadia in her arms. She was very annoyed that the boys were so late.

'Do you know how many million people there are in Cairo?' she asked Uncle Khalid sharply. 'If you arrange to meet one of these millions at a certain time and place, you've got to be there, otherwise how are you ever going to find them?'

Mother took them to the Mausoleum where Imām Shāfi'ī, the great Muslim scholar, was buried. It was a huge building and inside Muslims were walking round and round the tomb, reciting prayers from the Qur'ān.

The Shaikh – the religious man of the Mosque – joined them and explained that Imām Shāfi'ī was a very important person in early Islamic history because he established the Shāfi'ī school of *fiqh* (jurisprudence) which is one of the four well-known Islamic schools.

Imām Shāfi'ī came from a poor family and was brought up in Makkah, the Shaikh told them. When only seven years old he learnt the whole of the Qur'ān by heart. He became interested in Islamic law *(Sharī'ah)* which says what is right *(Ḥalāl)* and what is wrong *(Ḥarām).* Muslims try to follow the right path in everyday life. Imām Shāfi'ī spent years learning and teaching law in Makkah, Madinah and Iraq. When he later moved to Egypt, everyone realized what a brilliant teacher and lawyer he was, and how generous to the poor. In due course, his explanations of various aspects of Islamic law came to be known as the Shāfi'ī school. Other schools of *fiqh* are known after their founders, such as Ḥanafī, Mālikī and Ḥanbalī.

'Sadly, Imām Shāfi'ī died in Old Cairo on the last day of Rajab, 204 AH (20 January 820 CE),' finished the Shaikh, 'and his burial place is something of a shrine. The people walking round the tomb have come from all over the Muslim world to receive blessings and good health (known as *Barakah*) from the holy site.'

'I'm not sure that Muslims should believe in receiving blessings from anyone other than Allah,' said Mother thoughtfully, as the Shaikh left them. 'There is only one holy site that all Muslims want to visit and that is the *Ka'bah* at Makkah.' The *Ka'bah* is the house built by the Prophets Ibrāhīm (Abraham) and Ismā'īl (Ishmael) (peace be upon them). The boys had heard a lot about it and agreed that nothing could compare with making the Muslim journey, called *Ḥajj,* to Makkah.

3

Celebrating *'Īd al-Fiṭr*

That evening, Grandfather had a surprise for the boys as he had invited their student friend 'Alī to *Ifṭār,* the evening meal. It was a splendid occasion, being the meal to break the final fast of Ramaḍān. Aunt Samirah and Uncles Khalid and Hasan were impressed by 'Alī's knowledge of the Qur'ān and soon engaged him in a lively debate on Qur'ānic law.

At eight o'clock the Cairo sky was set ablaze as thousands of fireworks exploded into the air with loud cracks.

'*Al-Ḥamdulillāh*! The new moon has been sighted! *Kullu sanah wa antum ṭayyibīn*! (Many happy returns)' cried Father. The festival of *'Īd al-Fiṭr* had begun and Ramaḍān was over. Crack, crack! went the fireworks, and the streets filled with people rushing out to join in the festivities. 'Alī and the boys ran downstairs to join the throng, as excitement filled the night air.

As part of the festivities, there was a special 'sound and light' show that night at the pyramids, and Mother decided that they should all go to see it. It was a wonderful spectacle. Although Adam had glimpsed the immense man-made pyramids from the aeroplane, they seemed much larger from the ground, and truly impressive when illuminated against the night sky, still exploding with fireworks. Then the giant spotlight turned on the sphinx – a huge stone lion with a man's head. It looked quite frightening when lit up against the night sky.

Sound and Light at the Pyramids in Giza, Cairo

'The pyramids were built as tombs for the pharaoh rulers of Egypt many years ago,' 'Alī explained to Adam. 'It was in the days when Tutankhamun was king. This was long before the Holy Qur'ān was revealed to the Prophet Muḥammad (peace be upon him). The rulers of ancient Egypt ignored many prophets that Allah sent to guide mankind, and they refused to believe in the Oneness of Allah. They worshipped things like the sun, wrongly thinking that it was a god.'

'How silly. Surely no-one in Egypt worships the sun these days, do they?' asked Adam.

'No, for Allah in His Mercy has treated Egypt kindly,' 'Alī replied. 'His True Word reached us when the Muslims brought Islam here.'

'When did this happen?' asked Adam.

'Well, a man called 'Amr bin al-'Āṣ turned up with an army of Muslims in the year 639 CE,' said 'Alī, who knew a lot of history. 'Soon the Egyptian people accepted Islam because they realized that it was the One True Faith. Tomorrow I can take you to see the Mosque that 'Amr bin al-'Āṣ built.'

'So the pyramids and monuments of ancient Egypt have nothing to do with our Faith?' pondered Adam.

'No, but in any case we Egyptians are proud of what our ancestors achieved,' replied 'Alī.

The next day was filled with festivities. Adam was

overjoyed when cousin Yasmin and Aunt Zinah and his friend Fatimah turned up to visit them for the day.

'I haven't seen you since last summer!' said Adam in delight. 'How are things on the farm? Come and see my baby sister Nadia!'

As they played with little Nadia, Fatimah and Yasmin told Adam all the news from the Delta where the farms were. The goat had three new kids and the water buffalo had a calf this year, and Yasmin had helped to plant fifty small fruit trees the day before.

While everyone queued to use the showers, the children talked non-stop. At last it was time to put on their very best clothes to go to *Ṣalāt al-'Īd.* All the Mosques were overflowing with worshippers, so the whole family gathered with hundreds more in a big park where they lined up on their prayer mats facing Makkah. The words of the *Imām* were relayed to them by loudspeaker. Adam had never before seen so many people offering *Ṣalāt* (prayers) together.

After *Ṣalāh* everyone exchanged greetings and the children found themselves being hugged enthusiastically by complete strangers.

'*Kullu sanah wa antum ṭayyibīn*!' and *'Īd sa'īd*' they said.

Afterwards, they went back to the apartments where lots of friends including 'Alī dropped in to wish them ' *'Īd sa'īd*' (Happy *'Īd*) and they all exchanged gifts.

'Come on!' said 'Alī, excitedly. 'The fairground will be

open now. I'll treat you to some rides!' The children raced off with him to join in the fun. There were so many people at the fair that it was like a party.

'It's not only in Cairo that Muslims are celebrating *'Īd al-Fiṭr,'* said 'Alī, sitting next to Adam in a dodgem car. 'The whole Muslim world is celebrating today.'

Yasmin and Fatimah were enjoying themselves very much and encouraged the boys to go on the Big Wheel time and time again until Ahmad was looking decidedly green.

'Give us a break, Yasmin!' he groaned. 'I feel terrible!' But Yasmin and Fatimah only laughed and begged 'Alī to let them have just one more ride.

Next, 'Alī kept his promise to take the children on a trip round Cairo. They visited the Museum of Islamic Art and then went to the bustling Khān al-Khalīlī bazaar where Adam bought leather sleeping mats for the next day's camel safari. 'Alī took them up a rocky hill overlooking Cairo to visit the beautiful white Muḥammad 'Alī Mosque which towers above Cairo as big as a palace. Full of energy, 'Alī told them the history of everything, and later they all joined Mother and Father at the Mosque of 'Amr bin al-'Āṣ.

'This was the first Mosque in Egypt,' said Mother, reading from her guide book. 'To begin with, they used palm tree trunks for columns and the roof was thatched with palm leaves.'

'Alī didn't need a guide book. He told the family all about

how the Arab general ‘Amr bin al-‘Āṣ build the Mosque after bringing Islam to Egypt.

‘All Mosques were built in a very simple way at first,’ he said. ‘Can you imagine it, with just palm trunks and leaves? It was much later that Mosques were to be built in very grand styles, like the Muḥammad ‘Alī Mosque which we saw earlier.’

Father and Mother, who were setting up touring holidays in Egypt, were very impressed with ‘Alī’s knowledge.

‘We’re here in Cairo to plan our tours and decide which Islamic monuments our guests would like to see,’ Father explained to ‘Alī. ‘Our guests will all be Muslim families. Mother and I would like you to be our tour guide.’

‘Alī said he’d be delighted to be a guide. After offering their prayers in the Mosque, he said, ‘I hear from Adam that you’re all off on a trip to the Western Desert tomorrow.’

‘Yes, we’re going to test-run a camel trek and boat ride before we include them in our tours,’ said Father.

‘Well, *Rabbunā ma‘akum* – may Allah be with you all,’ said ‘Alī kindly, as they joined Mother and the girls coming out of the women’s part of the Mosque.

Next, ‘Alī whisked the cousins off to see more of the sights. They squeezed onto an overcrowded bus for a few stops and disembarked right beside the River Nile. They strolled along, watching hundreds of small boats plying the waters. The day was so hot and dusty that before long they started to wilt.

'I can't walk any further,' stated Muhammad at last. They were crossing a bridge to a large island in the river, and all five children were footsore.

'Don't worry, we'll stop for an ice cream at the top of Cairo Tower,' said 'Alī genially. 'After all, it is *'Īd al-Fiṭr* and everyone's celebrating.' They were thrilled as a lift carried them 610 feet to the top of the tower.

'What a view!' exclaimed Adam as they walked around the observation platform at the top. 'We can see the whole of Cairo from here! Just look at all those spires!'

'They are called minarets – Mosque towers,' said 'Alī, looking over the shoulders of the cousins.

'There must be lots of Mosques in Cairo, then,' observed Yasmin. 'I can see hundreds of minarets.'

'Yes, just a glance at all those minarets tells you that this is a Muslim city,' agreed 'Alī. 'We people of Cairo are glad of this.'

The city's history could be traced on the panorama below and 'Alī tirelessly explained and pointed out everything for the cousins. The River Nile dominated the view, sweeping northwards through the city and encircling the island where their tower stood. They sat down to strawberry ice creams, thankful for the cool refreshment.

'I'd never find my way around Cairo on my own,' decided Adam. 'Thanks for showing us around, 'Alī. It's been great.' 'Alī had been a good companion to them, and as they said goodbye to him back at the apartments, they promised to meet up again after their desert trip.

4
Desert safari

The desert stretched out before them – hundreds upon hundreds of miles of sandy, rocky desert. It looked like a sea of sand.

'This desert is known as The Great Sand Sea,' Mother remarked. 'Now we can see why.'

'Yes, the sand dunes are like waves in the sea,' said Muhammad.

Everyone was excited to see the haze of Cairo's dusty sky disappearing far behind them while the desert reached endlessly to the horizon and far beyond. Every window of the bus mirrored the same view: hot, shimmering desert, baking under the clear, blue Egyptian sky. Adam slid his window open and watched a long line of camels tramping slowly across the landscape, each one roped to the one in front.

'*Inshā' Allāh,* this time tomorrow, we'll be travelling like that!' he said with anticipation. His cousins Ahmad and Muhammad peered out of the windows eagerly. They were pleased to be visiting the desert with Adam and his parents and baby Nadia. It would be quite an adventure.

Presently, the bus stopped at a small roadside store where all the passengers bought bottles of water and glasses of sugar-cane syrup. It was time for *Ṣalāt al-Ẓuhr,* so the family joined other passengers in *Wuḍū'* at a washing area next to the store. They then made their prayers in a thatched enclosure where plaited reed mats were laid out on the floor. Adam wondered if the Mosque of 'Amr bin al-'Āṣ with its palm tree pillars, had been something like this. How different it was from the grand Mosques of Al-Azhar ash-Sharīf and Muḥammad 'Alī, and yet *Ṣalāh* itself was essentially the same.

'A Mosque needs only to be a space set apart for people to pray while facing Makkah,' said Father afterwards.

The bus bumped and jolted along the desert road on into the afternoon. It seemed that there was no end to this desert, but, at last, just as Adam was dozing off, an oasis came into view.

'*Al-Ḥamdulillāh*! An island of life in the sea of desert sands!' cried the bus driver poetically, as welcome greenery became visible at the bottom of the valley ahead.

The Oasis of Bahariyah looked to Adam just as an oasis should do: lush and green. He half expected to see a caravan of camels drinking thirstily around a water hole, but as they approached he realized that the oasis was far more than a water hole. It was an entire valley of greenery, and people had been living there for generations. There was a large lake flanked by tall date palms and knobbly olive trees, and among orchards of peach and orange trees were white-painted houses.

Their rest-house was next to the lake, so Adam and his

cousins ran down to the jetty even before they had unpacked. How good it was to stretch their legs after the hot journey!

'Look how many ducks there are!' said Ahmad. 'I wonder how they got here.'

'Maybe they were always here, they hatched here,' suggested Adam. 'They certainly couldn't have flown across the desert because it's too far. Look at them sitting on the boats!'

From the road some children shouted greetings to the boys in the local dialect. They were singing and laughing as they rode their donkeys at a leisurely pace. Maybe they were of the Bedouin people that Adam had heard live in the desert.

Evening came suddenly as the sun sank below the tree-lined horizon, turning the surrounding desert into fiery colours, while long plumes of desert dust looked like red smoke against the sky. Suddenly, hundreds of ducks took to the air from the lake and flew noisily back and forth across the valley three times.

As they settled on the lake once more, with much splashing and quacking, Father joined the boys on the jetty.

'Mother's just feeding Nadia and giving her a bath,' he said, paddling his fingers in the water. 'I wonder if there are any fish in this lake. Apparently all the water comes from a huge underground well beneath the desert.'

'Oh, is the lake man-made then?' asked Muhammad.

'No, it's quite natural,' said Father. 'The water comes up on its own from the rock below, which is called an aquifer. There are some hot water springs here, too.'

The family spent the evening excitedly discussing the next day's camel trek.

'I can't wait to see the camel I'll ride!' said Adam to Ahmad. 'Can Nadia ride with me, Mother?'

'I shouldn't think so,' said Mother laughing. 'But as none of us has ever ridden a camel before, it's hard to say who she'll be safest with.' But Nadia, rolling on the rug and kicking her legs, clapped her hands and chuckled. She didn't mind whose camel she went on.

In the evening before everyone went to bed, Father read to the family from the Qur'ān. He always said that no day is complete without reading from the Qur'ān. He helped the boys to memorize a new *sūrah*.

'We must put our whole hearts into reciting (or *Tilāwah*),' he said. 'Because what we read in the Qur'ān is the word of Allah which He has given us in human language.' Father went on to say how *Ṣalāh* – obligatory prayer –

commits to heart the *sūrahs* that make up the Qur'ān. No *sūrah* has changed in any way since the very beginning.

'The Holy Prophet (peace be upon him) used to recite the Qur'ān before Angel Jibra'īl (Gabriel) once during every Ramaḍān,' said Father. 'We too should memorize as much of the Qur'ān as we can.'

'But it's so much to remember!' said Muhammad. 'I could never memorize so much.'

'Then don't try to learn too much at once,' said Father. 'It is no good reading the Qur'ān quickly and without stopping to understand. The Holy Prophet (peace be upon him) was said to prefer to recite a short *sūrah* such as *al-Qāri'ah* with proper understanding than to hastily finish long ones such as *al-Baqarah* and *Āl 'Imrān.*'

Then Father read to them one of the often recited verses from *Sūrah al-Baqarah,* known as *Āyat al-Kursī*:

> Allah, the Ever-Living, the Self-Subsisting by Whom all subsist, there is no god but He. Neither slumber seizes Him, nor sleep; to Him belongs all that is in the heavens and all that is in the earth. Who is there who might intercede with Him save with His leave? He knows what lies before men and what is hidden from them, whereas they cannot attain to anything of His knowledge save what He wills them to attain. His Dominion overspreads the heavens and the earth, and their upholding wearies Him not; He is All-High, All-Glorious.
>
> (Verse 255 from *Sūrah al-Baqarah,* known as *Āyat al-Kursī,* the Verse of the Throne).

5

Camel trekking

At dawn, the Muezzin awoke Adam and he accompanied the rest of the family to the Mosque for *Ṣalāt al-Fajr*. The beautiful words of the Qur'ān seemed more than ever significant to Adam that morning. Feeling spiritually refreshed after prayers, the family then assembled outside the rest-house to help their camel guide, Idris, pack the baggage camel. Idris fastened their kit bags, tents and mosquito nets to the pack camel until the tall animal was quite heavily laden. Finally, he slung pairs of goatskin water containers over the camel's hump and helped the children to mount their waiting riding camels.

Each camel knelt in the sand while the children climbed onto the padded saddles.

'These camels only have one hump! I thought that camels should have two,' remarked Father, holding Nadia as Mother's animal rose to its feet.

'Not the Meharée camel of Arabia,' said Idris. 'One hump is enough,' he added obscurely. 'Are we ready?' Without waiting for a reply, he hissed to his camel and the others, roped together, set off after Idris's lead camel at a jolting walk.

'Oh, I'm going to fall off!' shouted Adam, alarmed to be so high off the ground.

'So am I! My saddle's not tied on properly!' cried Ahmad in a panicky voice.

'Hey, just calm down!' smiled Idris, turning in his saddle to glance at the newcomers to camel riding. 'Just take it easy, boys! You have to learn to sway with the camel.'

As Idris didn't seem inclined to give any further advice, Adam held on to the pommel of his saddle and tried to accustom himself to the curious swaying gait of the camel. He felt rather precarious. It was quite unlike riding a donkey or a pony.

'No wonder they call the camel the "Ship of the Desert" ' said Adam to Mother. 'I feel as though I'm out in the Channel in a dinghy! I just hope I don't capsize!'

The group travelled slowly towards the rocky hills bordering Bahariyah Oasis. Idris explained that his family were Bedouin people.

'Bedouins are tribes of wandering, or nomadic, people,' he said. 'Our people have lived in the deserts of Arabia since before living memory.' A minute later, as they rounded a large sand dune, they came upon Idris's family camping in a large leather tent. A number of goats and floppy-eared sheep nibbled at spiny shrubs nearby. The camels came to a halt as Idris's wife Zahra greeted the party.

'*As-salāmu 'alaikum*' she said, helping Mother and Nadia down from their camel. 'Come into the tent out of the sun. I expect you're feeling hungry?' They followed her into the tent, feeling wobbly and unsteady after their first camel ride. Sitting on plaited mats, Idris's three young

daughters were engrossed in playing cat's cradles with beaded strings.

'*As-salāmu 'alaikum*!' they said together, jumping up as their visitors appeared. The eldest girl, Sabāh, wearing a red dress and striped trousers, handed round soft biscuits. 'They're called "*harīsah*" ' she told Adam. 'And my sisters have made this cake which you must try too. We call it *mishabik*.'

Sabāh immediately organized a game for the boys and her sisters. 'Here we are, everyone takes a pencil and a sheet of paper,' she said. 'Now I describe an object and you all have to try to draw it. The first one to guess what it is wins. Ready? OK – draw a triangle.'

'I think it's an Egyptian pyramid,' guessed Adam.

'Clever you, right first time!' said Sabāh. 'It's your go now Adam.' Adam thought for a moment and then started to describe a bus. Sabāh interrupted him when he mentioned that it had wheels.

'You're not allowed to say "wheels" or "windows" or anything like that,' she scolded. 'You have to say "circles" and "squares" and so on, otherwise it's too easy.' Soon the children were absorbed in their game, and although they squabbled loudly over the rules, Nadia fell asleep on a sheepskin rug, undisturbed by the noise.

Idris busied himself checking the camels' backs to make sure that the saddles had not caused any sore patches, and he then made his guests glasses of mint tea. Adam thought the green brew looked awful, but tactfully avoided drinking any by saying that he wasn't a tea drinker. Zahra then gave both Adam and Nadia cups of goats' milk. Waking up, Nadia gurgled happily as everyone made a fuss of her.

'Are they your sheep and goats outside?' Muhammad asked Idris curiously.

'Yes, *Al-Ḥamdulillāh,* we are nomadic herders,' replied Idris. 'We tend our flocks and travel from oasis to oasis, trading a little and finding pasture for the animals.'

It sounded a wonderful way to live. Adam thought that it must be like being on holiday all the time.

The sun was creeping high in the sky, shortening the shadows and scorching the sand. The trekkers said goodbye to Idris's family and set off once more on their camels. Idris walked until they were under way, and then he mounted his camel by pulling its head down and kneeling on the bend in its neck. The camel straightened its neck and Idris landed lightly in his saddle. He was relaxed and unhurried in all his actions. He handed Mother a black umbrella to shade Nadia from the sun and pulled his white head-dress lower over his weather-beaten face.

'Make sure you give Nadia water from your flask every five minutes,' he instructed Mother, who was handing round the sun-block cream. 'We all need to drink a gallon of water a day in this heat. The temperature will reach 120 degrees today.' The air started to become hazy in the heat and the company fell silent as their small caravan moved steadily along a rocky camel path. All that could be heard was the occasional crick-crack of the camels' stiff joints as they picked their way over the rough ground on their soup-plate-like feet.

At last Idris called a halt on the ridge of a slope, and his camel knelt down at once in the shade of a boulder. Muhammad's camel followed suit and sank to its knees too with a gutteral groan which so startled Muhammad that he tumbled off, landing in the sand with a thud.

'Ouch! You could fry an egg on this sand!' he yelped.

'You look like a cat on a hot tin roof!' said Adam, scrambling down.

As it was time for *Ṣalāt al-'Aṣr,* they washed with bottled water and lined up their leather mats to face the direction of Makkah. They recited *Al-Fātiḥah* – the opening chapter of the Qur'ān, silently and it seemed to hold a special message for them on their travels.

> Praise be to Allah, the Lord of the entire universe,
> the Merciful, the Compassionate,
> the Master of the Day of Recompense.
> You alone do we worship, and You alone do we turn
>   to for help.
> Direct us on to the Straight Way,
> the way of those whom You have favoured,
> who did not incur Your wrath,
> who are not astray.

Together, they knelt, then bowed, pressing their foreheads to the ground.

6

Adam and camel are missing!

After *Ṣalāh,* everyone gave a hand untying the bags from the pack camel, for Idris had chosen this spot as their camp site. They erected three goatskin tents in the shadows of the rocks.

'I can't think why we'll need tents,' said Adam, unpacking his kit bag.'Couldn't we just sleep in our sleeping bags under the stars, Idris?'

'Sometimes, yes. Today, no,' said Idris, without further explanation. But the boys pressed him until he said, 'I just have a feeling that you will need your tents before nightfall.' Then he lapsed into silence again, and the boys were fascinated. Why would they need the shelter of their tents in the hot desert? Only half an hour later, though, the reason became evident, as a hot breeze began lifting the sand in little gusts and swirling it along the ground. Soon the wind picked up, sending sand racing over rocks in rivulets, stinging their legs and hands.

'I have no idea how Idris knew there'd be a sand storm,' said Adam, impressed. 'We'd better take shelter, just as he predicted.' As they crowded into the tents, the camels lay down to sleep, resting on their bellies with their heads laid along one-another's backs. They closed their nostrils to keep out the sand and snored. The wind became stronger, lashing at the tents. Adam enjoyed the isolated feeling only nomads experience when sitting out a sand storm in the middle of a desert, miles from anywhere.

'How many miles do you think we've come today?' Father asked Idris.

'From *Ṣalāt al-Fajr* to *Ṣalāt al-'Aṣr,* with stops,' said Idris with a big sigh, as if such a question was tiring for him.

'Yes, but how many miles would that be?' Father pressed him. Idris gave him a sideways look and shook his head slowly.

'Miles? Kilometres? What does it matter?' he smiled. 'One mile follows another in the desert. It's all in Allah's hands. The desert is a place for peace and prayer and quiet thinking. The Holy Prophet (peace be upon him) spent a lot of time praying and thinking in peace and quiet. He used to do this in a cave in the hills outside Makkah. Away from the hustle and bustle of the towns, people can be pure in heart and closer to Allah, you see.'

As they huddled in the tent with the sand swirling outside, Idris told the boys more about the Prophet Muḥammad (peace be upon him).

'Allah sent many messengers to earth to show people the Right Way of life,' he said. 'They were called prophets and all had the same religion. There is only one God – Allah – and they knew this. Then Allah sent Muḥammad (peace be upon him) as His Last Messenger to complete the mission and organize all those who accepted His Word into one community of Muslim people. You are part of that community today.'

'How did the Prophet Muḥammad (peace be upon him)

know that he was a messenger for Allah?' asked Ahmad.

'Well, when he was quietly thinking and praying in a cave in Mount Ḥirā', he was visited by the Angel Jibra'īl,' said Idris. 'The Angel Jibra'īl told Muḥammad (peace be upon him) that he had been chosen by Allah as His Last Messenger. Muḥammad (peace be upon him) then received Allah's messages from the Angel Jibra'īl, and every word was written down in a book. That book is the Qur'ān. The Word of God.'

The sandstorm finished as suddenly as it had started. When they went outside they discovered that sand had drifted half-way up the sides of the tents. Mother put Nadia in her carrying sling and accompanied Father for a walk before the sun set, while the boys prepared a fire ready to barbeque their meal. Idris had brought along some goat cheese made by his daughters, and loaves of flat bread, olives, dates and dried meat. As the flames of the fire rose, sand flies appeared as if from nowhere and started to bite.

'It's a good thing we brought along the mosquito nets,' said Muhammad, swiping a fly off his arm. Soon it was time to eat.

'*Bismillāhir Raḥmānir Raḥīm,*' said Father.

As they began to eat, a group of friendly Bedouins with a flock of sheep joined them around the camp fire and shared their food. They seemed to know Idris, and started to sing and play tunes on their wooden flutes. After a while, Adam went with Idris to give the camels their baskets of millet.

'Surely there's one camel missing!' exclaimed Adam, suddenly noticing a broken tether rope trailing in the sand.

'Looks like one of them has gone "walkabout",' agreed Idris with a shrug. 'It's your camel, too, young Adam. *Mā lish* – never mind. Let's go and look for him.' Adam was very upset to think that his camel had run off, and he ran

after Idris down the hillside, shouting over his shoulder to the others.

'It's my camel! He's escaped!' Several of the visiting Bedouin followed Adam at a gallop. Muhammad picked up one of their flutes and played a few tuneless notes on it.

'Shush! You'll scare away the sheep next!' scolded Mother. 'I wonder if Idris has experienced runaway

camels before? It could have gone miles for all we know and it's dark now.' The family watched anxiously for signs of the search party returning with the errant camel, but nothing was to be seen or heard.

At length, it was Father, standing guard over the remaining camels, who saw some lights bobbing about in the darkness. He thought that they were some way off, but actually they were quite close. They were the paraffin lanterns of Idris and his friends.

'No sign of the camel,' said Idris, returning to the camp fire. 'Where's Adam?'

'We thought he was with you!' said Mother, panicking at once. 'Let's call him. He must be lost!' Everyone started to feel alarmed, imagining Adam wandering in the darkness of the endless desert. What a dreadful experience that would be!

'*Inshā' Allāh,* Adam will turn up,' said Idris unworriedly, turning his attention to the barbeque. 'Who'd like a kebab?'

'Why does he have to be so relaxed about everything!' grumbled Mother. 'Fancy thinking about a kebab at a time like this!' She was about to organize a search party when a scrunch-scrunch of footsteps was heard in the sand. It was Adam, together with the missing camel!

'*Al-Ḥamdulillāh*!, I found my camel!' announced Adam as Mother and Father hugged him in relief. 'He was at the bottom of the hill.'

'*Al-Ḥamdulillāh*!' said everyone together. 'I had a feeling you'd find him,' smiled Idris, handing round cups of cardamom coffee. Father and Mother there and then made a rule that no-one was again to wander away from the rest of the group during the camel trek. As they munched their kebabs round the camp fire, Father described how explorers could get lost in deserts. Idris used strips of palm leaves to plait a new rope for Adam's camel and told them tales of desert travellers, such as Ibn Baṭṭūṭah, who crossed the Great Sand Sea in days gone by.

'Did you know that the Prophet Muḥammad (peace be upon him), was no stranger to this kind of life?' asked Idris. 'He used to lead camel caravans in the deserts of Arabia.'

'Oh, I thought that the Prophet (peace be upon him) was a shepherd,' said Muhammad the cousin of Adam.

'Yes, he was a shepherd, but that was when he was just a lad,' replied Idris. 'He used to tend sheep on the outskirts of Makkah. Later, his uncle Abū Ṭālib started taking him on trading journeys by camel and when he became experienced at handling camels, the Prophet (peace be upon him) led caravans himself. The camels actually belonged to a wealthy widow called Khadījah, and she and the Holy Prophet (peace be upon him) eventually got married.'

The family offered their final prayers of the day, *Ṣalāt al-'Ishā',* and read together from the Qur'ān until it was time for bed.

Lying in his sleeping bag next to Muhammad and Ahmad

that night, Adam stared into the darkness, listening to the silence of the desert. 'Isn't it cold?' he whispered. 'I'm glad we've got such warm sleeping bags.'

'I know, and it was so hot today that I couldn't imagine ever needing a pullover again,' agreed Muhammad. 'I'm surprised how quiet it is, too,' he mused. 'It's almost too quiet, isn't it?'

'Not really. In Cairo it's so noisy you can hardly hear yourself think!' whispered Ahmad.

'But if you listen really carefully, you can still hear little sounds,' Muhammad said, propping himself up on to one elbow to listen. 'I can hear the camels munching.'

'Yes, and I can hear Nadia gurgling in Mother and Father's tent,' said Adam.

'You can understand why the Prophet (peace be upon him) wanted to get away from the noisy city to ponder in the cave,' thought Ahmad. 'Hey – I hope there are no snakes around here! I've heard about someone waking up to find a snake sleeping on his feet!'

'How awful,' said Adam, shuddering. 'But I've fixed the mosquito net all round the opening of the tent. I'm sure no snake could get in. Apparently it was the insects that made my camel run off – they were annoying him so much.'

Content that there were neither snakes nor insects in their goatskin tent, the boys drifted into sleep, dreaming that they were riding their camels.

7

Trekking to the oasis

They awoke at dawn to hear the camels growling amongst themselves. It was time for *Ṣalāt al-Fajr,* and they performed *Wuḍū'* in refreshingly chilly water.

After morning prayers, the boys sat sleepily on their leather mats around the fire. Father had collected enough dried scrub to keep the fire going for a few minutes while Muhammad made tea and Idris heated up several tins of *fool medammes* beans.

'*Bismillāhir Raḥmānir Raḥīm.* A perfect way to start the morning,' Idris said, passing round bowls of steaming food. For Nadia, he had collected a mug of fresh, warm camel milk, and she gulped it down thirstily. 'You'll all feel lively in a minute,' said Idris, regarding the sleepy family with amusement. 'Then we can strike camp before the sun gets up.' This seemed to be a good idea, although the camels didn't appear to be in a hurry to go anywhere. They were still lying down, and even Idris had problems persuading the pack camel to get up.

Very soon there remained not a trace of the night's camp site and the party was on the move once more. Ahmad and Muhammad complained of aching legs and stiff backs after yesterday's jolting ride, so Idris cushioned their saddles with the sleeping bags to make the riders more comfortable.

'Maybe your camels are feeling stiff, too, after carrying you yesterday!' joked Idris. 'It is important to keep the camels comfortable, and that's why I put padding under the saddles to stop their backs from rubbing sore. That's also why you have to take off your shoes and just wear socks when you're riding.' Then Idris started to chant from the Qur'ān verses which concern the importance of animals.

> He created the cattle. They are a source of clothing and food and also a variety of other benefits for you.
>
> And you find beauty in them as you drive them to pasture in the morning and as you drive them back home in the evening;
>
> and they carry your loads to many a place which you would be unable to reach without much hardship. Surely your Lord is Much-Loving, Most-Merciful.
>
> And He created horses and mules and asses for you to ride, and also for your adornment. And He creates many things (for you) that you do not even know about.
>
> (*Sūrah an-Naḥl* 16: 5–8)

'I hope you understand the meaning of these verses,' said Idris, clearly in an expansive mood. 'Allah in His Mercy and Kindness has given us animals which we must be good to. The Qur'ān tells us to be compassionate and kind to all people and animals. All Muslims must remember this. Our camels, for example, are very important to us. We make robes and blankets from their hair and we drink their milk. Most of all, our camels carry us and our belongings across the desert, so this has meant that for thousands of years people have been able to travel from one land to the next.'

Without pack animals, Idris went on to tell them, the medieval Muslim traveller Ibn Baṭṭūṭah, one of history's great explorers, would not have set out from Morocco to make the Pilgrimage of *Ḥajj* to Makkah and far, far beyond. He crossed the desert not too far from where they were now.

'I suppose there were no cars or trains in those days?' surmized Adam.

'Of course not – the "Land Rover" of the Middle Ages was the camel!' said Idris. 'In some parts of the Sahara, camels are still used regularly for transport.'

The air was cool and clear as they trekked downhill. Bahariyah Oasis came into view set in the valley floor below, looking as remote as a mirage.

'You wouldn't know that we were in the modern world,' commented Ahmad after a while. 'The Age of Technology and all that.'

'I know, I almost expect to see characters from the *Arabian Nights* appearing over the hilltops,' said Adam. 'I wonder what has changed since Ibn Baṭṭūṭah was travelling this way?' he speculated.

As though in answer to his question, the reality of the present-day world was brought home to them when they reached a row of ugly concrete houses. A soldier dressed in khaki uniform appeared and signalled them to stop.

'This is a military area,' he announced sternly. 'You should keep moving and not stop or take any photographs!' As he looked at the family's passports and papers, Adam wondered what there could be in this part of the desert that was so important that it should not be photographed. It didn't look any different from the rest of the desert, except for the army trucks and the soldiers wandering around. Adam had to suppress a sudden mischievous urge to get out his camera.

'I can't imagine what secrets there are here,' said Adam to Father as they continued. 'It just looks like desert to me.'

'Ah well, looks can deceive,' said Father. 'Just think of the Valley of the Kings where all those tombs have been found . . . '

' . . . the tomb of Tutankhamun?' asked Adam at once. 'We did a project on him at school. He was a king of ancient Egypt and was buried with all his treasures, which we saw in the museum in Cairo.'

'That's correct,' said Father. 'There are burial chambers of lots of other kings too and no-one thought that the desert valley hid such things. So you never know!'

As they topped the ridge of a tall dune, the desert fell away dramatically on the rim of the valley. Below lay the sparkling lake and cultivation of the oasis. They wound their way down, going from sand to soil.

The tired party reached the oasis just as a noisy wedding procession was parading down the main street. Hoards of women swarmed around a pretty young bride, singing and clapping in celebration. It was really very noisy, but the camels refused to be startled and tramped on steadfastly until they reached the rest-house.

'*Al-Ḥamdulillāh*! A safe return,' said Idris, helping everyone to dismount. It was time to bid Idris and the camels a reluctant farewell. They had really enjoyed the camel trek.

8

A fright in the night

A Muezzin started to call the *Adhān* (call to prayer) from the tall minaret of the local mosque. It was time for *Ṣalāh*:

Allāhu Akbar Allah is great
Allāhu Akbar Allah is great
Allāhu Akbar Allah is great
Allāhu Akbar Allah is great
Ash-hadu an lā ilāha illa-llāh I bear witness that there is no god apart from Allah
Ash-hadu an lā ilāha illa-llāh I bear witness that there is no god apart from Allah
Ash-hadu anna Muḥammadar-rasūlu-llāh I bear witness that Muḥammad is Allah's messenger
Ash-hadu anna Muḥammadar-rasūlu-llāh I bear witness that Muḥammad is Allah's messenger
Ḥayya' 'alas-ṣalāh Come to prayer
Ḥayya' 'alas-ṣalāh Come to prayer
Ḥayya' 'alal-falāḥ Come to salvation
Ḥayya' 'alal-falāḥ Come to salvation
Allāhu Akbar Allah is great
Allāhu Akbar Allah is great
Lā ilāha illa-llāh There is no god apart from Allah.

As he heard the *Adhān* five times every day, Adam knew the words by heart. While walking with the family down the lane to attend *Ṣalāt al-'Ishā',* he asked Father about the *Shahādah.*

'One of the duties of all Muslims is to say the *Shahādah,'* replied Father. 'The words of the *Shahādah* are included in the *Adhān,* which we've just heard. So they are easy to remember:

' "I bear witness that there is no god apart from Allah and I bear witness that Muhammad is the messenger of Allah".'

The Mosque was full of people waiting to pray. As always, the *Imām* stood at the front of the Mosque facing Makkah and everyone followed him exactly as he said the prayers.

Afterwards, they returned to the rest-house, only to find that there was a power-cut, so they went to bed in the dark. In the pitch-black of their room, Adam and his cousins were alarmed to hear scuffling noises nearby. There was a rustle and a shuffle and then another rustle. Eventually they could bear it no longer and Ahmad found a torch in his kitbag and shone it around the room feeling rather scared. Suddenly he burst out laughing, startling the others, for the noisy culprits turned out to be nothing more sinister than a couple of doves roosting on top of the wardrobe.

Adam left the shutters open so that the doves could come and go as they pleased.

'I was quite frightened for a minute,' admitted Muhammad at last. 'Let's see if we can remember the verses of the

Qur'ān which the Holy Prophet (peace be upon him) said will keep away harm at night.' It was the last two verses of *al-Baqarah* and the boys read it together by torchlight.

> The Messenger believes, and so do the believers, in the guidance sent down upon him from his Lord: each one believes in Allah, and in His angels, and in His Books, and in His Messengers. They say: 'We make no distinction between any of His messengers. We hear and obey. Our Lord! Grant us Your forgiveness; to You we are destined to return.'
>
> Allah does not lay a responsibility on anyone beyond his capacity. In his favour shall be whatever good each one does, and against him whatever evil he does. (Believers! Pray thus to your Lord): 'Our Lord! Take us not to task if we forget or commit mistakes. Our Lord! Lay not on us a burden such as You laid on those gone before us. Our Lord! Lay not on us burdens which we do not have the power to bear. And overlook our faults, and forgive us, and have mercy upon us. You are our Guardian; grant us victory, then, against the unbelieving folk.'
>
> (*Sūrah al-Baqarah,* 2: 285–6)

بِسْمِ اللّٰهِ الرَّحْمٰنِ الرَّحِيْمِ

اٰمَنَ الرَّسُوْلُ بِمَآ اُنْزِلَ اِلَيْهِ مِنْ رَّبِّهٖ وَالْمُؤْمِنُوْنَ ؕ
كُلٌّ اٰمَنَ بِاللّٰهِ وَمَلٰٓئِكَتِهٖ وَكُتُبِهٖ وَرُسُلِهٖ ۟ لَا نُفَرِّقُ بَيْنَ
اَحَدٍ مِّنْ رُّسُلِهٖ ۟ وَقَالُوْا سَمِعْنَا وَاَطَعْنَا ۗ غُفْرَانَكَ رَبَّنَا وَاِلَيْكَ
الْمَصِيْرُ ﴿٢٨٥﴾ لَا يُكَلِّفُ اللّٰهُ نَفْسًا اِلَّا وُسْعَهَا ؕ لَهَا مَا كَسَبَتْ وَعَلَيْهَا
مَا اكْتَسَبَتْ ؕ رَبَّنَا لَا تُؤَاخِذْنَآ اِنْ نَّسِيْنَآ اَوْ اَخْطَاْنَا ۚ رَبَّنَا وَلَا
تَحْمِلْ عَلَيْنَآ اِصْرًا كَمَا حَمَلْتَهٗ عَلَى الَّذِيْنَ مِنْ قَبْلِنَا ۚ رَبَّنَا وَلَا
تُحَمِّلْنَا مَا لَا طَاقَةَ لَنَا بِهٖ ۚ وَاعْفُ عَنَّا ۟ وَاغْفِرْ لَنَا ۟ وَارْحَمْنَا ۟
اَنْتَ مَوْلٰىنَا فَانْصُرْنَا عَلَى الْقَوْمِ الْكٰفِرِيْنَ ﴿٢٨٦﴾ ع

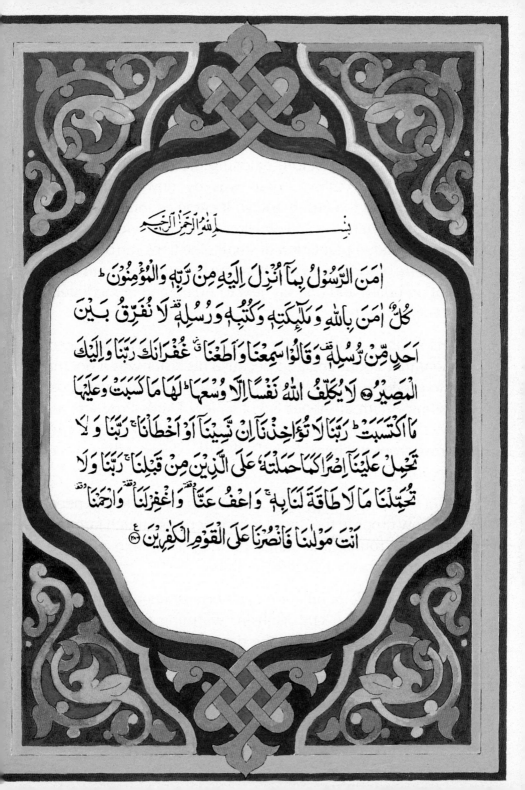

9

Sailing on the Nile

The next morning after *Ṣalāt al-Fajr* it was time for a hurried breakfast before catching the desert bus bound for the Nile Valley. Adam was by now used to the emptiness of the desert and so it came as something of a surprise when a small village came into view on the desert road. A plantation of small pine trees surrounded a large rig of some kind and here the bus stopped. Four men got on board and one sat next to Adam and immediately started chatting.

'*As-salāmu 'alaikum,* I'm Muhsin,' he said. He asked Adam all about England because his sister was a doctor there. Muhsin himself was an engineer and he was soon telling Adam all about Egypt's New Lands Programme. 'We're drilling for water in the desert so that people can grow crops out here. *Inshā' Allāh,* the desert will become green!'

'But that seems a big task,' said Adam. 'Why do you need to grow crops in the desert when there's so much farming land all round the banks of the River Nile and the oases?'

'Egypt's whole population can't be sustained on the river banks for ever,' said Muhsin, warming to his subject. 'There's lots of space in the desert, though! Farmers are being given animals and money to farm the desert at places where we find underground water. *Al-Ḥamdulil-lāh,* anything's possible! Allah, in His Wisdom, has given us the intelligence to find solutions to problems, so that's what we're trying to do.'

Adam tried to imagine the barren desert with corn and fruit trees, with farmers tilling the soil. It seemed so unlikely, yet what determination and ingenuity the Egyptians could show! '*Inshā' Allāh,* your scheme will be successful,' he told Muhsin.

Later in the day, they reached the great River Nile flowing slowly northwards between its lush green banks.

'Well, this is it!' said Father, jumping out of his seat eagerly. 'Our sailtrek is about to begin!' Father, at home on boats, quickly led the family down to a jetty where their white sailing boat (called a *felucca*) was waiting for them.

Their skipper, Husni, moved barefoot about the boat with the grace of a cat. He soon had the whole family seated on board, and gave lifejackets to Nadia and the boys before unfurling a tall triangular sail. The broad river was quiet and calm, but the boat made little splashing noises as it sped along, sailing alongside a mid-stream island.

'I can see some white birds on the island!' said Adam, sitting near the bows.

'They'll be egrets,' informed Husni, looking into the distance. 'You'll see plenty along the way because they aren't alarmed by sailing boats.'

Just then, a large paddle-steamer chugged past, swirling up the water. Adam decided that it was much nicer to

glide along the river in a silent *felucca* than to be on a noisy river-boat. As they sailed on, Husni put up a white canopy to shade them from the sun, and he then invited the boys to take his position holding the long tiller at the boat's stern. Husni squatted comfortably on the very edge of the boat as he demonstrated how to push the wooden arm of the tiller from one side to the other.

'Look, the tiller moves the rudder under the water, causing the boat to turn,' he said, handing the tiller to Adam. 'Have a go.' It took a minute or two to get accustomed to steering the boat, but Adam quickly decided that sailing was easier than camel riding. Ahmad wanted a go next, but when he took the tiller, he pushed it so hard that the boat turned in a circle and the sails started to flap.

'You've turned us into the wind' said Husni, taking over. 'Watch out for the boom – the wooden arm on the bottom of the sail – it can swing across the boat quite suddenly.' He was very patient and let the boys take turns at the helm all afternoon. Nadia sat in the bow with Mother and Father, shrieking with delight when she saw children on the river bank giving a black water buffalo a bath.

The banks of the river were full of life. They passed a tanning centre where men were dipping sheepskins in earthenware vats of dye. A boy cooking a catfish over a fire waved to them as they passed a rice field sparkling with water. They watched two men turning the handles of irrigation pumps to disperse the river water over the fields. Women planting rice chatted to each other and sang along with the music on their transistor radio. Mother spotted five or six babies sleeping in string beds, or hammocks, swinging gently in the shade of some lemon trees.

Soon the familiar cry of a Muezzin calling faithful Muslims to prayers resounded in the air. Hearing this, Husni headed for the shore and moored the *felucca* at the jetty of a village. Obeying the call to prayer, they attended *Ṣalāt al-'Aṣr* at a white Mosque in the village.

The local people were very friendly and showed the boys round a family-run workshop. The jugs they made were exported to Britain as part of Egypt's Productive Families Project. The family was then invited to a meal at the house of Shaikh Hasan, who had conducted the prayers. He and his wife plied their visitors with fried *ta'miyah* and creamy goats' milk curds, and asked all about their trip.

Shaikh Hasan knew the whole of the Holy Qur'ān by heart, and he talked to Adam and his cousins about it.

'Do you know why the Qur'ān is a unique book?' he asked.

'Yes, it's because it's a book revealed by Allah Himself,' said Adam promptly. The Shaikh was satisfied with this answer.

'The Angel Jibra'īl, acting on the instructions of Allah, revealed the Qur'ān to the Prophet Muḥammad (peace be upon him) over a number of years,' he told the boys. 'The aim of the Qur'ān is to guide people in their lives, and you should read some of the Qur'ān every day.' Shaikh Hasan explained that there are five things that Muslims, as obedient servants of Allah, are particularly asked to do. They are to say the *Shahādah*; to pray five times a day; to fast in the month of Ramaḍān; to pay *Zakāt* (charity) to the needy; and, if possible, to go on a pilgrimage to Makkah.

'What exactly happens in Makkah?' asked Adam. In reply the Shaikh described how over a million Muslims from all over the world come together on the site of the *Ka'bah* – the original house built in Makkah by the Prophet Ibrāhīm (peace be upon him) and his son Ismā'īl (peace be upon him). During *Ḥajj,* which takes five days, pilgrims spend certain days in special prayers and rituals. They put on white clothes called *Iḥrām* and journey from Makkah to Minā. The next day they go to a place called 'Arafāt and spend the day there in prayer. Everyone leaves 'Arafāt at sunset and spends the night at Muzdalifah before returning to Minā the next morning. Pilgrims circle seven times around the *Ka'bah* because it serves as a symbol of unity for all Muslims. The pilgrims also walk between the two hills of Ṣafā and Marwah which are near to the *Ka'bah* and sacrifice animals in Minā.

'It's called the pilgrimage of *Ḥajj* and it makes every pilgrim pure and clean in the eyes of Allah,' said the Shaikh. Both he and his wife were known as *Hājjis* because they had completed *Ḥajj.*

'*Inshā' Allāh,* we will all be *Hājjis* one day too,' said Adam thoughtfully.

Before they left, the Shaikh's wife presented them with a huge basket of delicious fruit and fresh bread.

'All produce of our village,' she said proudly. 'We give thanks to Allah for His blessings.'

Eager to resume their journey, Adam and Ahmad were first back to the jetty. Five children were jumping about all over the boat.

'Can you sail us to the opposite bank?' they begged Adam. 'The river ferry doesn't cross today.' Husni strolled up and agreed to take the young passengers, and their faces lit up with smiles. Two of the little girls played with Nadia, threading flowers in her curly hair and making her laugh. When they reached the bank, the children leapt to their feet and thanked everyone over and over again for the lift before racing up the river bank to where their mother was supervizing a water buffalo turning a water wheel.

'*As-salāmu 'alaikum*!' cried the children. '*Rabbunā ma'akum* – may Allah be with you on your journey!'

10

An island campsite

The day was drawing in as Husni steered the *felucca* onto the muddy shoreline of a river island dotted with date palms.

'This is our campsite for tonight,' he announced. Adam, Muhammad and Ahmad jumped ashore at once, delighted to find that they were the only people on the island.

'It's wonderful!' said Adam appreciatively. 'Where shall we put up the tents?'

'No need for tents,' smiled Husni. 'Tonight you sleep under the stars!' This seemed even better, and in no time, Husni had secured string hammocks between the palm trees.

'I don't know why we don't always sleep in hammocks!' said Ahmad, swinging comfortably in his. '*Al-Ḥamdulillāh,* I could live a life on the river.'

As it was time for *Ṣalāt al-Maghrib,* Husni glanced at the setting sun and then the hour hand of his watch to determine the direction of Makkah.

'We must face in this direction,' he said, pointing. They washed themselves ready for prayer and then Husni asked, 'Do you know what the Qur'ān has to say about washing for prayer?' Then he recited:

Believers! When you stand up for Prayer wash your

faces and your hands up to the elbows, and wipe your heads, and wash your feet up to the ankles.

(*Sūrah al-Mā'idah* 5: 6)

Father led the prayers under the date palms that evening. Afterwards, Husni took the boys fishing, and they caught five large Nile perch which they grilled over a camp fire for supper.

Chewing one of the dates that Shaikh Hasan had given them, Adam asked Husni if he spent all his time sailing.

'No, not really,' Husni said to their surprise. 'I'm a health worker and most of my time is taken up with a vaccination programme around here. But I also use this *felucca* to transport pottery along the Nile to the export centre at Asyut.'

As the camp fire died down, the night set in and after *Ṣalāt al-'Ishā'* they decided to retire to their hammocks. Husni covered each hammock with a mosquito net, and Mother tucked Nadia snugly in the sleeping bag with her. The balmy night was alive with the noice of cicada insects and croaking bullfrogs. In the distance a water buffalo gave a melancholy bellow.

The next thing Adam knew, Husni was gently shaking his hammock. 'Time for *Ṣalāt al-Fajr,*' he said. Adam couldn't think where he was for a moment. Was he in the desert? Ah, no, he was on a tiny island with the great River

Nile flowing all around. As he climbed down, a loud thud told him that someone had fallen out of his hammock.

'Ouch!' came Ahmad's protest in the darkness. 'It's not so easy to get out of a hammock, is it! Hey, I'm all tied up in my mosquito net!' His eyes now accustomed to the dark, Adam went to help unravel his cousin from the net, and then they went to meet Husni at the prayer site. After *Ṣalāt al-Fajr,* Husni suggested that they should start the day's journey because there was a slight breeze and they could make good headway. This agreed, they packed up the hammocks and all scrambled aboard the *felucca,* Mother carrying Nadia, who was fast asleep. Husni pushed the boat into the gently rippling water, hopping lightly across emerging stones before leaping into the stern without so much as getting his feet wet.

The river was inky dark, the stars overhead the only lights, yet Husni took the helm with confidence. A light breeze filled the sail and the family fell silent as the water slosh-sloshed rhythmically against the bows. Husni watched quietly as one by one his passengers pulled their sleeping bags around themselves and dozed.

11

A swarm of bees

Adam awoke to find himself looking at the shadow of a white heron which was sitting on the canopy above him. 'I must have slept for hours,' he yawned, stretching. He helped himself to a mango from the fruit basket and leafed through Mother's bird book. Sitting on his heels by the tiller, as motionless as the heron, Husni was effortlessly steering the boat with one hand.

'Look! Isn't that a crocodile?' said Adam in excitement, pointing to a long dark shape in the water ahead. 'It's coming towards us!' Ahmad and Muhammad were beside him at once, unsure whether to be frightened or curious.

'Sorry to disappoint you, but there aren't any crocodiles around here,' said Husni with a smile.

'But there must be! I've heard of the Nile Crocodiles,' protested Adam. 'And I'm sure that's one of them!' But Husni shook his head, and he was right after all, for it was only a log floating in the water. 'You'd have to follow the River Nile south of the Aswan Dam to meet the Nile Crocs,' said Husni. 'I don't think that log is going to snap us up!'

The sun was up and the voices of children reached them as a riverside village came into view on the near bank. Husni announced that it was time for a break, so Father jumped ashore to moor the *felucca* and then the boys climbed out, helping Mother with Nadia. Almost as soon as they arrived, scores of people came to meet them, greeting them enthusiastically, and laughing and joking with Husni. Evidently he was well known here.

'I'm going to visit some colleagues in the Health Centre,' he told Father. 'Would you like to come?' They followed Husni along the paths of the village to a smart new hospital. Here Husni introduced the family to a team of doctors and nurses.

'We're in the middle of an immunization programme,' said a lady doctor. 'But there have been a lot of patients suffering from bee stings this week too. You have to watch out for bees when they're on the move,' she warned.

Just as they left the clinic, the sky darkened ominously as a huge swarm of bees buzzed overhead. Husni acted swiftly, pushing everyone through the door of the nearest building, which turned out to be a bakehouse.

'That was lucky!' said Mother, holding Nadia tightly in her carrying sling. 'There must have been thousands of bees all flying together!' They sheltered for a minute until the hum of the bees had faded away.

The village baker welcomed them and showed Adam and his cousins how bread was baked. Flat slabs of dough were folded and kneaded and finally slapped onto the inside walls of a giant stone oven, and left to bake. Not only bread was baked here, for Adam spotted local women coming into the bakery carrying their family meals, ready to cook.

'It's a communal kitchen, really,' said the baker.

'*Al-Ḥamdulillāh,* our ovens are always hot, so everyone comes to use them. Allah provides, and so we share what we have.'

'What an excellent idea,' said Mother, clearly impressed. 'We should do something like this in England.'

Outside the bakehouse an old man was carving an intricate pattern on a circular piece of wood. He was painstakingly carving in beautiful Arabic script the opening chapter of the Qur'ān – *Sūrah al-Fātiḥah.* The script went round and round and the man said it would take him ten more days to complete. They all admired his patience and dedication. Father bought a finished carving to put up on the wall at home in England.

After *Ṣalāt al-Ẓuhr* they climbed aboard the *felucca* for the final leg of their sail down the Nile. Adam relaxed in the back of the boat, drinking in the peace and quiet of the surroundings. Later, at the railway station waiting for the train to take them back to Cairo, it was time to say goodbye to Husni.

'It's been brilliant. We've made many friends on this journey,' said Adam.

'Well, that's what life is,' smiled Husni. 'A journey. *Rabbunā ma'akum* to you all – may Allah be with you on your journeys wherever you go.'

'*As-salāmu 'alaikum,*' they said to Husni, and as the train pulled out of the station, the whole family turned to wave to their friend. *Inshā' Allāh* they would meet him again some day.

GLOSSARY

ABD AL-BĀSIṬ 'ABDUS ṢAMAD, QĀRĪ: Well-known Qur'ān reciter from Egypt.

ABŪ ṬĀLIB: The uncle who brought up the Prophet Muḥammad (peace be upon him) from the age of eight.

ADHĀN: The words of the Muezzin when calling Muslims to prayer.

AKENKATEN (1372\1354 BC): King of Egypt who worshipped the sun and was husband of Queen Nefertiti.

AL-ḤAMDULILLĀH: Expression used by Muslims to give thanks to Allah.

'AMR BIN AL-'ĀṢ: A Muslim general who brought an army to Egypt in 639 CE and established Islam among the Egyptian people.

ANGEL JIBRA'ĪL (GABRIEL): The angel who, acting on the instructions of Allah, revealed the words of the Holy Qur'ān to the Prophet Muḥammad (peace be upon him). Angels are created by Allah and carry out His orders.

ANTIQUITIES: Objects from times long gone by. Egyptian antiquities include treasures, jewellery, and works of art of the Pharaohs.

AQUIFER: Rock which holds a large store of water. Much of the Middle East relies on aquifers for fresh water in areas far from rivers.

AS-SALĀMU 'ALAIKUM: Muslim greeting to wish someone peace. The reply is *WA 'ALAIKUM AS-SALĀM,* meaning 'and peace be upon you, too'.

ASWAN DAM: Huge dam, completed in 1972, which controls the flow of the River Nile in Egypt and behind which is Lake Nasser (310 miles long).

ĀYAT AL-KURSĪ: Verse 255 of *Sūrah al-Baqarah,* known as the Verse of the Throne. It is one of the most beautiful verses of the Qur'ān.

BAHARIYAH OASIS: Lush area in the Western Desert with many sites of historical interest including catacombs, Roman ruins and bas reliefs.

AL-BAQARAH: The second *sūrah* (chapter) of the Qur'ān with 286 verses. It describes how Ibrāhīm and Ismā'īl (peace be upon them) built the *Ka'bah* and founded Islam.

BARAKAH: Luck or blessing, usually in connection with a holy person or place.

BEDOUIN: Arab people of the desert who traditionally move from place to place with their camels, flocks of sheep and goats.

CAIRO: The 1,000-year-old capital of Egypt situated on the banks of the River Nile, founded by the Fātimids and now one of the most densely-populated cities of the world. The city has numerous beautiful mosques with tall minarets raised to the glory of Allah.

CAIRO TOWER or al-Burj: On Gezira (Island) in the River Nile in central Cairo, this 187m.-high tower is a popular recent landmark from the top of which there is a wonderful view.

EGYPTIAN MUSEUM OF ANTIQUITIES: Situated on Shāri' Mariette in Cairo, it houses the world's finest collection of treasures from Egypt's past, including the golden mask of the boy-King, Tutankhamun.

FAST: A period of time during which someone goes without food and drink. Muslims fast during the daytime in the month of Ramaḍān; it is one of the five Pillars of Islam.

AL-FĀTIḤAH: The opening *surāh* (chapter) of the Qur'ān, which sums up the essence of the Qur'ān. Its seven beautiful verses are repeated at every *Ṣalāh*.

FĀTIMIDS: Muslim people from North Africa who claimed to be descended from the Prophet Muḥammad (peace be upon him). They seized Egypt, making Cairo the capital of their caliphate in 968 CE. They founded Al-Azhar ash-Sharīf University and made Cairo a great cultural centre. The Fātimid empire finally fell in 1169 CE.

FELUCCA: Boat with a large triangular sail.

FOOL MEDAMMES: A traditional savoury bean dish eaten with bread for breakfast.

GALABAYAH: A traditional savoury bean dish eaten with bread for breakfast.

ḤAJJ: The pilgrimage to Makkah as explained by the Prophet Muḥammad (peace be upon him); one of the five Pillars of Islam. All Muslims must complete *Ḥajj* if they are able to.

HĀJJĪ: A Muslim who has completed *Ḥajj.*

ḤALĀL: Something which is allowed in Islam.

ḤARĀM: Something which is not allowed in Islam.

HARĪSAH: Sticky kind of sweet biscuit/pastry.

HOLY PROPHET (peace be upon him): Another way of referring to the Prophet Muḥammad (peace be upon him).

IBN BAṬṬŪṬAH: A 14th-century Muslim scholar and explorer from Morocco who for nearly 30 years travelled 75,000 miles through Africa and Asia. He made several pilgrimages (*Ḥajj*) to Makkah.

IBRĀHĪM (ABRAHAM): A Prophet (peace be upon him) greatly blessed by Allah who taught that there is no god but Allah. He had two sons who were also Prophets: Ismā'īl and Isḥāq (peace be upon them). Isḥāq's son Ya'qūb (peace be upon him) was also a Prophet. The Prophet Ibrāhīm and his son Ismā'īl (peace be upon them) built the *Ka'bah* in Makkah which was blessed by Allah and is the oldest house of prayer in the world.

'ĪD AL-FIṬR: Muslim festival marking the end of Ramaḍān.

'ĪD SA'ĪD: Islamic greeting, meaning 'Happy *'Īd*'.

IFṬĀR: Meal which is eaten at the end of a fast (period without food and drink).

IḤRĀM: The seamless clothes worn by pilgrims doing *Ḥajj*. The clothes give everyone the same status, whether they are rich or poor, as all people are equal before Allah.

IMĀM: Person chosen to lead *Ṣalāh.*

IMĀM SHĀFI'Ī: Muslim scholar who founded a school of Islamic law. In Sunni Islam there are four rites (or *Madhhabs*): the Shāfi'ī, Ḥanafī, Mālikī and Ḥanbalī.

ĀL 'IMRĀN: Third *sūrah* (chapter) of the Qur'ān with 200 verses, giving the story of 'Imrān, the father of Mūsā (peace be upon him).

INSHĀ' ALLĀH: Meaning 'if Allah wills it'.

ISLAM: Submission and obedience to Allah. Islam also means peace because accepting Allah's commands brings peace. One who accepts the Islamic way of life is a Muslim.

ISMĀ'ĪL (ISHMAEL): Prophet who together with his father, Prophet Ibrāhīm (peace be upon them) built the *Ka'bah*.

KA'BAH: In Makkah, the world's oldest prayer house, founded by the Prophet Adam and built by the Prophet Ibrāhīm and his son Ismā'īl (peace be upon them all). Blessed by Allah, it is the focus of the Islamic world, acting as a symbol of unity towards which all Muslims face in prayer. Pilgrims walk seven times around the *Ka'bah* during *Ḥajj* and *'Umrah*.

KHADĪJAH: The first wife of the Prophet Muḥammad (peace be upon him). An intelligent and noble lady, she was a widow aged 40 when she married the Prophet (peace be upon him). They had six children, and Khadījah became the first person to accept Islam after her husband.

KHĀN AL-KHALĪLĪ: Alive with bustle and excitement, this oriental bazaar in Old Cairo, a maze of alleys and passages, is a treasure-trove of goods of every description. As well as being one of the largest, it is also among the oldest bazaars in the world, dating from the 14th century CE.

MADRASAH: School or place of study.

MADRASAH AND MOSQUE AL-AZHAR ASH-SHARĪF: Meaning 'the most radiant', it was founded in 970 CE as the principal Mosque of the new Fātimid city of Cairo. Built by Jawhar, commander-in-chief of the army of al-Mu'iz li-Dīnīllāh, it was named after Fāṭimah, daughter of the Prophet (peace be upon him). It is one of the oldest

Islamic universities and has a reputation as a centre of excellence in many subjects.

AL-MĀ'IDAH: Fifth *sūrah* (chapter) of the Qur'ān.

MĀ LISH: Arabic expression for 'never mind'.

MAUSOLEUM: Building in which a person is buried after death.

MIḤRĀB: An alcove in the wall of every mosque which indicates the direction of Makkah and of prayer.

MINARET: Tower from which the call to prayer is given five times a day.

MISHABIK: Sticky cake in the form of a lattice structure.

MOSQUE: Place where Muslims come together for prayer.

MOSQUE OF 'AMR BIN AL-'ĀṢ: In the Old Coptic Quarter of Cairo, it was the first mosque built in Egypt and the fourth in the world. Repairs and additions have been made over the years to the original structure (built in 642 CE), which was of palm-tree trunks with a roof of palm leaves.

MOSQUE AND MAUSOLEUM OF IMĀM SHĀFI'Ī: Named after Imām Abū 'Abdullāh Muḥammad ibn Idrīs al-Shāfi'ī, the founder of one of the four Islamic schools. His mausoleum is one of the oldest of its kind and the Mosque is known for its large dome.

MOUNT ḤIRĀ': The revelation of the Qur'ān began in 610 CE at Ḥirā'. In a cave, the Angel Jibra'īl revealed the words of the Qur'ān to the Prophet Muḥammad (peace be upon him).

MUEZZIN: One who calls Muslims to prayer fives times a day.

MUḤAMMAD 'ALĪ MOSQUE or Alabaster Mosque: Sited on the fortress of Saladin (Ṣalāḥuddīn). Built between 1830 and 1849 in an Ottoman Baroque style and faced with white alabaster, it dominates the skyline.

MUSAHHARATĪ: Crier who awakens Muslims during the month of Ramaḍān so that they can eat before the day's fast begins at dawn.

MUSEUM OF ISLAMIC ART: Situated in Ahmed Maher Square near to the Al-Azhar Mosque, it houses a very fine collection of art objects (e.g. wooden lattice-work and ceramics) from Persian, Mamluk and Turkish schools.

MUSLIM: Person who accepts and acts upon the Islamic way of life in obedience to Allah.

AL-NAḤL: Sixteenth *sūrah* (chapter) of the Qur'ān.

PHARAOH: Ruler or King of ancient Egypt famous throughout the world for building pyramids, temples and tombs.

PILLARS OF ISLAM: The five things that Muslims must do: to say *Shahādah*; to pray five times a day; to fast during the month of Ramaḍān; to pay *Zakāt* to the poor and, if possible, to go on a pilgrimage to Makkah.

PROPHET: Man specially chosen by Allah to deliver His Message to the people on earth. There have been many Prophets: Adam was the first and Muḥammad (peace be upon them both) the last.

PROPHET MUḤAMMAD (peace be upon him): Allah's last Prophet to whom the Qur'ān was revealed.

PYRAMIDS OF GIZA: Together with the Sphinx, these are the last surviving of the Seven Wonders of the World. Huge, towering structures, they were built by three of the Pharaohs: Cheops, Chephren and Mycerinos at Giza near Cairo around 5000 years ago. Serving as tombs for kings, they are known the world over as hallmarks of Egypt.

AL-QĀRI'AH: Short (11 verses) *sūrah,* No. 101, describing the Day of Judgement.

QUR'ĀN: The Word of Allah as revealed to the Prophet Muḥammad (peace be upon him) and later written down as a book, which is the basis of Islam.

RAMAḌĀN: Ninth month of the Islamic year. It is one of the Pillars of Islam that healthy adult Muslims must fast during daylight hours for the days of Ramaḍān. There are twelve months in the Islamic calendar, based on the phases of the moon and moving forwards by about 11 days each year.

RAMSES II: Pharaoh from 1304–1237 BC, he organized the building of gigantic monuments in Egypt including the temple at Abū Simbal with four 60-feet high stone figures of himself.

RIVER NILE: Longest river in the world, measuring 4145 miles (6670km.). It flows through much of Africa before reaching Egypt, where it finally branches out into a delta to meet the Mediterranean Sea. The life-giving waters of the Nile are vital to Egypt.

ṢALĀH: The prayer offered to Allah using words and actions as shown by the Prophet Muḥammad (peace be upon him). The five daily *Ṣalāh* are: *Fajr, Zuhr, 'Aṣr, Maghrib* and *'Ishā'*. Special *Ṣalāh* include *Ṣalāt'ul Jumu'ah* on Fridays and *Ṣalāt 'Īd al-Fiṭr.*

SHAHĀDAH: The first Pillar of Islam which is a declaration of Faith in the Oneness of Allah and that Muḥammad (peace be upon him) is His messenger.

SHAIKH: Religious man connected with the Mosque who knows the entire Qur'ān by heart and devotes his time to Islam.

SHARĪ'AH: Islamic law laid down in the Qur'ān, providing a code of conduct for Muslims. The word *Sharī'ah* means clear, straight path.

SOUND AND LIGHT: A unique evening performance when lights are shone on the three pyramids and the Sphinx while the history is broadcast (in four languages) together with atmospheric music.

SPHINX: Huge, ancient statue sculptured to look like Pharaoh Chephren with a lion's body.

SUḤŪR: Meal eaten before daybreak during Ramaḍān to provide Muslims with the strength to carry out the day's fasting.

SŪRAH: Chapter of the Qur'ān. There are 114 *sūrahs* in the Qur'ān.

TĀHIR SQUARE: Large and busy traffic interchange near the River Nile in Cairo.

TA'MIYAH: A delicious and very filling dish of spicy, mashed beans, fried and often eaten hot for breakfast.

TASBĪḤ: The praising of Allah with the use of repetitive phrases, performed (optionally) after *Ṣalāh*.

TILĀWAH: Reciting verses from the Holy Qur'ān.

TUTANKHAMUN: Boy-King of ancient Egypt who died when he was just 19 years old. He was buried in a tomb which was discovered in 1922 and which contained 1,700 items of treasure, many of which are on display in the Egyptian Museum, Cairo.

VALLEY OF THE KINGS: On the western bank of the Nile, the location of tombs of Pharaohs of the 18th, 19th and 20th dynasties. The Pharaohs were buried, with all their treasures, in decorated, secret, sealed passages.

WUḌŪ': The special way in which Muslims wash before praying to make themselves pure and clean.

ZAKĀT: The duty of Muslims to pay 2.5% of their wealth once a year to the poor so that money is spread more evenly in the community. *Zakāt* is one of the five Pillars of Islam.